DEL & ZIAH

The Friendly Wolf Pups

Once upon a time, while the rest of the pack was sleeping. Ziah woke up and could hear a faint voice from far away. It sounded like someone was crying out for help. She stuck her head outside of their cave and started slowly walking towards the faint voice. She looked up at a tree branch and heard the owl hoot "Hoo, Hoo." As she kept walking, she got startled and saw several bats flying toward the moon. "This is scary," Ziah said to herself. She decided to keep walking towards the voice and jumped over a big rock.

Ziah found an old turtle on its back screaming: "Help! Someone, please help me." "I can help you, Mr. Turtle," said Ziah.

She used her paws to gently turn the turtle right side up. "Oh, thank you, my dear," said the turtle. "It's my pleasure to help you, Mr. Turtle," said Ziah.

"Call me Joe! I've been yelling for a long time and you were the only one that could hear me" said the turtle.

"ZIAH!" yelled the mommy wolf frantically looking for her pup. "I'll be right there mama, I was helping out my new friend Joe the turtle," said Ziah.

Ziah said goodbye to Joe the turtle and ran towards her mama. "Where were you?" said the mommy wolf. "I couldn't sleep because I could hear someone was in trouble," said Ziah. "That's a very nice thing to help others, but you are too little to wander off on your own. It can be dangerous! Please don't do it again." said the mommy wolf. "Okay, mama," said Ziah. Ziah and her mama went back to the cave and fell asleep.

The next day, the pack went to a nearby farm to get some fresh fruits and vegetables. Suddenly, Del wandered off from the pack and found an old dog who looked very sick. "Excuse me, Mr. Dog, are you ok?" said Del.

The dog coughed a few times before he was able to respond. "I've been very sick for a long time." "I can make you feel better Mr. Dog" said Del. Del gently put his paw on the dog's chest and closed his eyes.

A blast of white light surrounded them and within a few minutes, the dog started feeling better. "I don't feel sick anymore! Thank you so much" said the dog. "It's my pleasure to help you, Mr. Dog," said Del. "Call me Rocky," said the dog.

"DEL!" yelled the daddy wolf frantically looking for his pup. Del said goodbye to the dog and ran towards his daddy. "Where were you?" said the daddy wolf "I was helping out a sick dog," said Del. That's a very nice thing to help others, but you are too little to wander off on your own. It can be dangerous! Please don't do it again." said the daddy wolf. "Okay, daddy," said Del.

The pack started walking back home with plenty of fruits and vegetables from the farm. Suddenly, three big angry-looking bears confronted the pack. "Give us your food, now!" said the biggest bear. "This is our food now get out of here and leave us alone," said the daddy wolf. "Well, it's ours now," said the big angry bear.

The three bears started running towards the pack to take their food. "HELP" yelled the mommy wolf. All of a sudden, Rocky and his brothers Lucky and Jasper, appeared with several of their friends from the farm. "Leave them alone right now, those are my friends," said Rocky.

The bears were surprised to see so many farm animals appear and started walking away from the wolf pack and all of their friends. Suddenly, the big bear tripped on something that looked like a rock and fell to the ground.

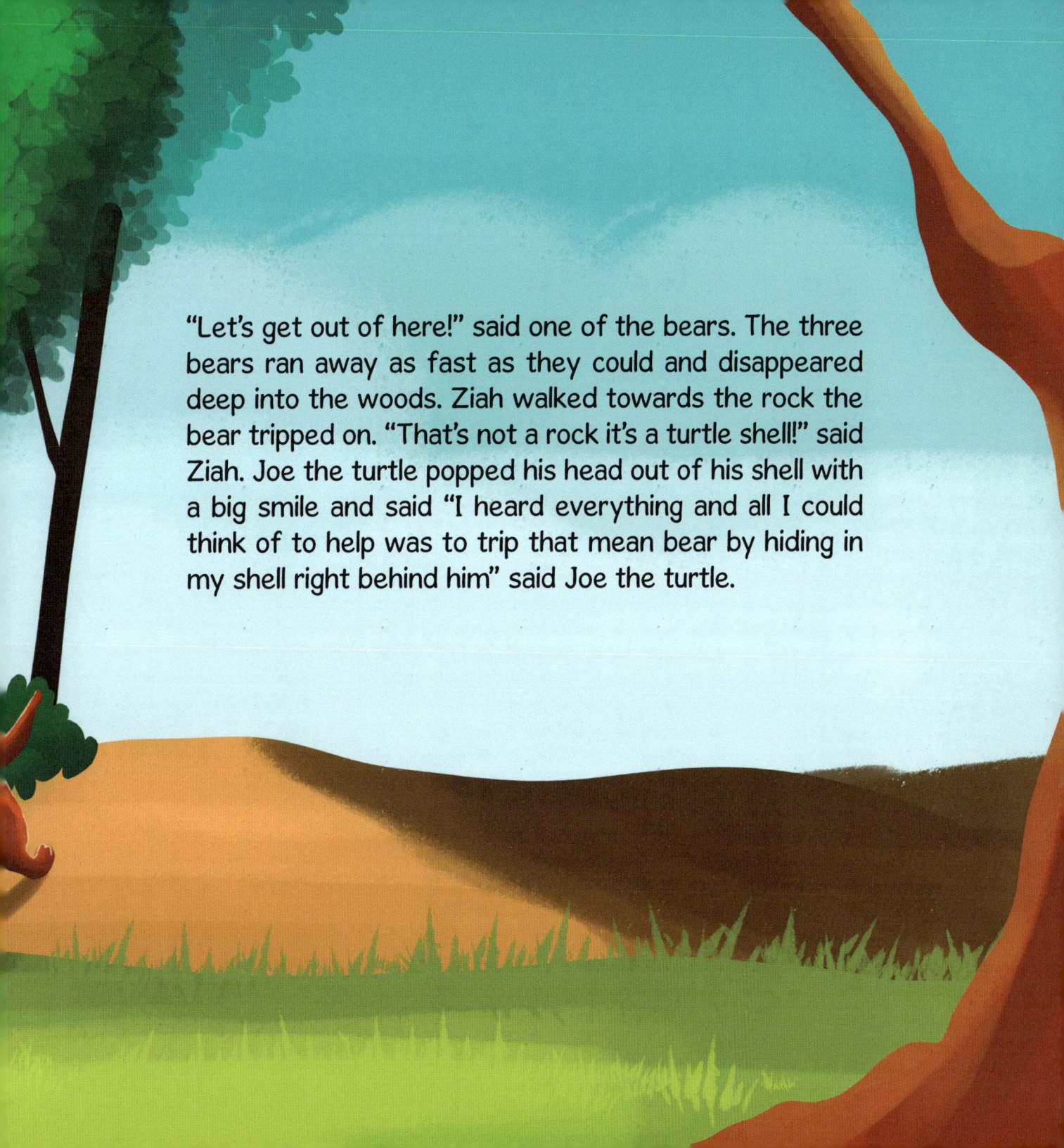

"Let's get out of here!" said one of the bears. The three bears ran away as fast as they could and disappeared deep into the woods. Ziah walked towards the rock the bear tripped on. "That's not a rock it's a turtle shell!" said Ziah. Joe the turtle popped his head out of his shell with a big smile and said "I heard everything and all I could think of to help was to trip that mean bear by hiding in my shell right behind him" said Joe the turtle.

"Thank you so much, Joe, Rocky, and all of your friends for helping us, "said the mommy wolf. "It's our pleasure," said Joe.

The wolf pack, Joe the turtle, Rocky, and all of his farm friends spent the rest of the day having a big picnic in the woods to celebrate and they lived happily ever after.

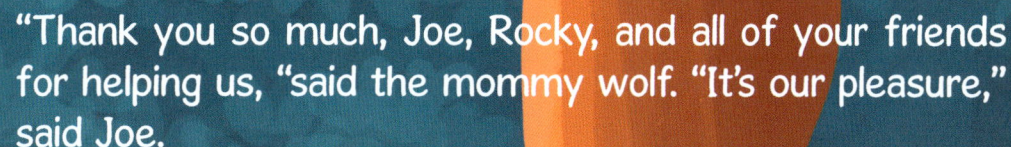

Printed in Great Britain
by Amazon